Special thanks to Liss Norton

For the Satwell family, with love. xxx

ORCHARD BOOKS
Carmelite House
50 Victoria Embankment
London EC4Y 0DZ
Orchard Books Australia
Level 17/207 Kent Street, Sydney, NSW 2000
A Paperback Original

First published in 2015 by Orchard Books

Text © Hothouse Fiction Limited 2015

Illustrations © Orchard Books 2015

A CIP catalogue record for this book is available
from the British Library.

ISBN 978 1 40834 010 3

1 3 5 7 9 10 8 6 4 2

Printed in Great Britain

The paper and board used in this book are made from wood from responsible sources

Orchard Books is an imprint of Hachette Children's Group and published by the
Watts Publishing Group Limited, an Hachette UK company.
www.hachette.co.uk

Series created by Hothouse Fiction
www.hothousefiction.com

Pixie Spell

ROSIE BANKS

ORCHARD

This is the Secret Kingdom

The Winter Wonderland Show

Contents

A Snowy Surprise

"My project's going to be about deep-sea creatures," said Ellie MacDonald excitedly. She and her friends Summer Hammond and Jasmine Smith were doing their homework in Summer's living room. They were working on projects about animal habitats.

Ellie flipped through the book she'd been reading until she came to a picture showing whales, sharks and fish. "I'll be able to write about all of these." She glanced at Summer's two little brothers, Finn and Connor, who were playing at the other end of the room, then lowered her voice. "Too bad I can't write about mermaids, but Mrs Benson will think I'm making them up."

Jasmine looked up from the computer screen and grinned. "I'm doing my project on desert animals, like camels." She added in a whisper, "But not the pink ones we rode in the Secret Kingdom."

The girls smiled excitedly at each other, thinking about the amazing secret they all shared. They often visited a magical land called the Secret Kingdom. It was ruled by kind King Merry and it was full of fairies, pixies, dragons and other wonderful creatures. During their last two adventures there they'd made friends with mermaids and ridden on pink camels!

"What habitat are you doing for your project, Summer?" asked Jasmine.

Summer sighed. "I just can't decide." She loved all animals and was finding it impossible to choose.

Finn and Connor started arguing over a train, shouting and snatching it from each other. "Anyway," Summer said with a giggle, "it's hard to think with those two squabbling."

"I wish we could move to the garden," said Ellie. "It's more peaceful out there." It was a beautiful summer's day and the girls were all dressed in shorts and T-shirts.

Summer's mum came in. "Whatever's going on in here?" she asked.

"Connor snatched the train off me," moaned Finn.

"I had it first," Connor wailed.

"Take it in turns," said Mum. "Ten minutes each. When the timer pings, you swap." She set the timer on her phone. "You can have it first, Finn, and your time starts…now!"

The girls exchanged anxious looks.

"Are you thinking about Queen

Malice's hourglass?" Jasmine whispered.

Summer and Ellie nodded. Queen
Malice, King Merry's mean sister, had put
a curse on the Secret Kingdom. As black
sand ran through her hourglass, all the
good magic was slowly being drained
out of the kingdom. When all the sand
was gone, the good magic would be lost
forever – and Queen Malice would take
over as ruler. The only way to lift the
curse was by bringing four Enchanted
Objects together again. The girls had
already found three of them, but it hadn't
been easy. King Merry's ancestors had
hidden the Enchanted Objects well, to
protect them.

"I wonder if King Merry's figured
out where the last Enchanted Object is
hidden," said Jasmine. It was still missing

and time was running out!

"I wish Trixi would send us a message," said Summer. Their pixie friend, Trixi, sent them messages through their Magic Box when they were needed in the Secret Kingdom.

"Me, too," Ellie agreed. "Let's check the Magic Box now."

"We're just having a quick break from our homework," Summer called to her mum.

The girls ran upstairs to Summer's bedroom.

Summer opened her wardrobe and a bright light shone out. "The Magic Box is glowing!" she cried excitedly. She lifted it out quickly and placed it on her desk. It was a wooden box, beautifully carved with mermaids, unicorns and

other magical
creatures. A
mirror was set
into the box's
lid, surrounded
by six green
gems.

The girls
crowded round the
box eagerly and Ellie
read out the words that
had appeared on the glowing mirror:

"This magical place is very high.
It's full of ice and snow.
Pixies build cute snowmen there,
And that's where you must go."

The box flew open and a magical map

of the Secret Kingdom floated
out. Jasmine caught it and spread it out
on the bed. Looking at the map was
usually like peering through a window
into the Secret Kingdom because the
figures on it moved. But today there were
no fluffy bunnies hopping around Cloud
Island or dolphins splashing in the sea
near Candy Cove.

"The map's not moving," Jasmine said, puzzled.

"It must be because of Queen Malice's curse," Summer said.

The Secret Kingdom's magic hadn't been working properly on their last three visits.

"We'd better solve the riddle quickly," said Ellie.

"We're looking for somewhere high and snowy," said Jasmine.

"Where pixies live," Ellie added.

They all bent low over the map, trying to read the tiny writing.

Jasmine spotted some mountains near the top of the map. "Mountains are sometimes covered in snow," she said. "And they're high." She squinted to read the writing more easily. "Look!

This place is called Pixie Peak!"

"That must be it," said Ellie. "Well done, Jasmine."

Summer folded the map and put it safely back inside the Magic Box, then they all touched the green gems on the lid.

"The answer is Pixie Peak," they all cried together.

The box opened and green sparkles came whirling out. Trixi was in the middle of them, zooming on her leaf. She was dressed in a cute purple cape edged with white fur. The hood

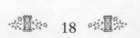

was pulled up, hiding her tiny pointed ears and her blonde hair. On her dainty feet were matching fur-lined boots with curly toes. "It's lovely to see you all!" she exclaimed. She flew to each of the girls in turn and kissed them on the tips of their noses.

"It's good to see you, too, Trixi," said Summer. "But I can tell your magic still isn't working properly."

"How?" Trixi asked, surprised.

"You're dressed for winter," Summer pointed out, "and it's boiling today!"

Trixi laughed. "We're going to the far north of the Secret Kingdom," she explained. "It's always wintery there. King Merry thinks the last Enchanted Object might be hidden there. Are you ready to go?"

The girls grinned. "Of course we are!" said Jasmine eagerly.

The girls joined hands then Trixi tapped her pixie ring and chanted:

"Off to Pixie Peak we'll fly,
Where mountains reach up to the sky."

Pink sparkles whooshed out of the ring and swirled around the room, lifting the girls off their feet.

"Secret Kingdom, here we come!" Summer cried.

ᵕPixie Peak ᵕ

As the girls landed gently in soft,
powdery snow, the magical pink sparkles
became a flurry of glittering white
snowflakes.

"We're here," Ellie said excitedly.

The snowflakes cleared and they
saw that they were in a snowy valley
surrounded by towering mountains. The
sky was brilliant blue and the sun shone

so brightly that the snow twinkled as though it was scattered with diamonds.

"What an amazing place!" breathed Jasmine.

Glancing down, the girls saw that they were wearing warm clothes, mittens and fur-lined boots like Trixi's. Jasmine had a long pink scarf wrapped around her neck, Summer had a fluffy yellow one and Ellie wore a furry sleeveless jacket. Beautiful jewelled tiaras rested on top of their heads. These always appeared when the girls arrived in the Secret Kingdom and showed that they were Very Important Friends of King Merry.

Trixi pointed to the tallest mountain. "That's Pixie Peak, the highest point in the whole kingdom. The Winter Pixies who live here are the smallest creatures in the realm. Let's go and meet some of them." She zoomed away on her leaf and the girls hurried after her, leaving footprints in the glistening snow.

"Look at the cute houses," Summer said, as they headed towards a little village nestling at the foot of the mountains. Sweet wooden chalets the size of dolls' houses had roofs covered thickly in snow. Colourful shutters framed the windows and smoke spiralled from the chimneys. Glittering icicles hung from beautifully carved balconies. Between the chalets, cheerful bunting fluttered in the gentle breeze.

"What's the bunting for, Trixi?" Jasmine asked. "Is something special going on?"

"The Winter Wonderland Show is today," replied Trixi. "I'm hoping my cousin Dusty will be here for it. I'm sure she'll be happy to help us find the last Enchanted Object."

They heard whooping behind them and turned to see a group of grinning pixies flying towards the village on pretty, lacy snowflakes.

"Winter Pixies ride snowflakes instead of leaves," Trixi explained.

More pixies went zipping past as they went into the village. The streets were full of pixies and the girls had to step carefully so they didn't tread on them.

"Now I know how giants feel," said Ellie, giggling and stooping down to peer into a tiny shop selling knitted hats and mittens.

Outside every building was a snowman.

"Hey, this one looks a bit like King Merry!" Summer exclaimed, spotting a snowman with twig arms and a crown made of snow. The girls gathered round to admire it.

Trixi tapped her pixie ring and a few sparkles drifted out of it and touched the snowman. It moved its twig arms jerkily, then stopped. Trixi sighed. "The snowmen are meant to come to life, but the magic's not working because of Queen Malice's spell."

All around the village pixies were tapping their rings, trying to bring their snowmen to life, but the snow figures barely moved.

"Their magic won't work unless Queen Malice's curse is broken," said Jasmine.

"So we'd better find the last Enchanted Object before the show," added Ellie.

As they went through the village, they saw young pixies throwing themselves down and swishing their arms and legs through the snow.

"What are they doing, Trixi?" asked Summer.

"They're making snow fairies," Trixi replied.

When the pixies stood up, the girls could see that their arms had made wings and their legs had made dress shapes in the snow.

The pixies tapped their rings. "I hope the magic works this time," said one. "My

snowman didn't move at all."

A few of the snow fairies flapped their wings weakly, then fell still again.

"Are they meant to fly?" asked Summer.

"Yes," Trixi replied, sounding worried. "Watching snow fairies fly is one of the best parts of the Winter Wonderland show."

In the village square they saw a
U-shaped dip in the snow.

"That looks like a skateboard ramp,"
Ellie said.

"Only pixie sized," added Jasmine.

A pixie suddenly came zooming across
the snow on her snowflake. She slid down
into the dip, then shot up the other side.
As she flew through the air, she did an
amazing double back flip. Unluckily, her
snowflake zipped out from underneath
her, and she landed on her back in the
snow.

"Are you all right?"
the girls called,
bending down
to help her
up.

"I'm fine,"

she said. "The snow gave me a soft landing!" Laughing, she sprang up and brushed loose snow from her clothes.

"Dusty!" cried Trixi, flying over to her.

"Trixi!" the Winter Pixie said, giving her a hug. "I hoped you'd come." She giggled. "I'm doing a flying display in the show, but my snowflake hasn't been behaving itself!"

"Nobody's magic is working properly because of Queen Malice's curse," explained Trixi.

Dusty sighed. "Oh dear. How can the

Winter Wonderland Show go ahead without magic?"

"We've come to look for an Enchanted Object to break the curse," said Summer. "We've found three already, and King Merry thinks the last one is hidden somewhere in the north of the kingdom."

"Do you have any idea where we should look?" Ellie asked hopefully.

Dusty wrinkled her nose thoughtfully, but before she could reply they heard the deafening roar of an engine behind them. Hearts pounding, they whirled round. A black object was hurtling towards them across the snow.

"Look out!" yelled Jasmine. She grabbed Ellie and Summer's hands and dragged them clear.

Trixi pulled Dusty to safety and they

all landed in a heap in the snow.

"What is it?" Summer said with a gulp as they struggled to their feet.

The black object skidded to a stop, showering them in powdery snow, and they saw that it was a shiny snowmobile being driven by a tall, thin woman dressed in black and wearing a crash helmet that covered her face.

She took off the crash helmet, releasing a frizz of wild black hair. The girls exchanged horrified looks.

"Queen Malice!" they groaned.

No Time to Lose!

Queen Malice climbed off her
snowmobile. "Ha! I thought I'd find you
pesky girls here!" she screeched. Smirking
nastily, she thumped her thunderbolt
staff down in the snow and her hourglass
magically appeared. To their horror, the
girls saw that almost all the black sand
had run through.

"Your time is nearly up," Queen Malice said. "Without the final Enchanted Object, the other three will be useless." She threw back her head and cackled, her hair bobbing furiously. "Soon the only magic left in the Secret Kingdom will be mine!"

She climbed back on to her snowmobile. "I'll leave you the hourglass, shall I?" she said, setting it down in the snow. "I wouldn't want you to lose track of time!" Laughing unkindly, she put on her helmet again and zoomed away, sending terrified Winter Pixies diving out of her way.

"Thank goodness she's gone," said Summer. "We've got to do whatever it takes to break her curse!"

They all turned to look at Dusty. "Can you think what the final Enchanted Object might be?" Jasmine asked.

"No," Dusty replied. "But I think I know *where* it might be hidden." She pointed to the summit of Pixie Peak. "There's a chalet at the very top of Pixie Peak. The scroll with the secret spell that gives the kingdom winter magic is stored there for safekeeping."

The girls exchanged hopeful looks.

"If the spell's *that* important, the scroll might be the Enchanted Object!" cried Summer.

They gazed up at the mountain top. It was a very long way to climb, but it was the only way to defeat Queen Malice.

"It's not just the climb that will be difficult," said Dusty, as though reading their minds. "The Hairy Snow Monster lives on the mountain." She shivered. "It's a huge, white, furry creature that prowls around the top of Pixie Peak. That's why we pixies live in the valley. Everyone's too scared to go up the mountain in case they meet the monster."

"We're not scared," said Jasmine bravely.

"And we don't have a choice, anyway. We've got to find the last Enchanted Object!"

"I'll come with you," Dusty said, squeezing Trixi's hand. "It's not just Pixie Peak's magic at stake — the whole of the Secret Kingdom will lose its magic forever if Queen Malice gets her way!"

"We'd better get going," said Summer

in a determined voice.

"Definitely," Ellie agreed, glancing at the hourglass. "The sooner the better!"

The girls set off, with Trixi and Dusty flying along beside them. There was no path to follow, just a soft quilt of glittering snow that stretched up and up towards the peak.

At first the girls enjoyed tramping through the snow. The base of the mountain was a gentle slope and it was fun to make deep footprints in the crisp snow. They chattered happily as they climbed.

Before long the slope became steeper and the girls' legs began to ache. Here and there, jagged rocks jutted up through the snow. They skirted round most of them, but some they had to climb over.

The rocks
were slippery
and chilled the girls'
hands, even though they
were wearing thick mittens.

"Brr! It's colder up here," said
Summer with a shiver.

"And rockier, too," said Jasmine through
chattering teeth.

At last they came to a cluster of rocks
that were so steep they couldn't climb
over them.

"We'll have to go round," said Ellie,
"but it looks an awfully long way."

"Can you fly us to the top with your
magic, Trixi?" Jasmine asked.

"I'll try," replied Trixi, "but I'm not sure
my magic will be strong enough."

"I'll help, too," offered Dusty.

She and Trixi tapped their rings and
chanted a spell:

"These rocks are much too high and wide
So fly our friends to the other side."

The girls held their breath as pink
and silver sparkles whooshed out of
both pixies' rings and whirled around

them. They felt themselves being lifted off
their feet.

"It's working!" cheered Ellie.

But the magic only lifted them a few
centimetres off the ground before setting
them down again in exactly the same
place.

"Botheration!" Trixi tutted.

"Never mind," Jasmine said. "We'll just
have to keep on walking."

The girls trudged around the jutting
rocks. Summer glanced down at the
village. It was so far below them now
she could barely make out the Winter
Pixies preparing for the Winter
Wonderland Show.

"How far down the mountain does the
Hairy Snow Monster come, Dusty?" she
asked nervously.

"I don't know," replied Dusty. "Nobody's ever seen him. We just know he lives on the mountain top."

"We'd better watch out, then," said Summer. She lowered her voice. "Maybe we should be a bit quieter, so he doesn't hear us coming."

They carried on climbing in silence and soon they reached a gap in the chain of rocks.

"We can go through here," Trixi said, flying into the passage to investigate. "These rocks are on the edge of a sheer drop, but there's a big slab of stone that crosses the ravine like a bridge so we can get across."

Ellie gulped. She was afraid of heights and hated the idea of having to cross the narrow bridge. Trembling, she looked around, hoping to find another way across the ravine.

"Don't worry, Ellie," said Jasmine, taking her hand.

Summer held her other hand. "We'll help you," she said.

Ellie nodded anxiously, too frightened to speak.

"Here goes," said Jasmine, leading the way into the gap between the rocks.

Mustering all her courage, Ellie went next and Summer followed after her. Ellie didn't dare to look down. She kept her eyes fixed on the mountain's peak.

"You're doing really well," Summer called to Ellie encouragingly. She glanced down into the ravine as they crossed, trying not to gasp when she saw the jagged rocks a long way below.

Once they were all safely over the bridge, they found themselves on a steep, snowy slope that led right to the top of Pixie Peak. Fir trees and low bushes were dotted here and there and, beyond them, right at the top of the slope, they could see the chalet where the Pixie Spell scroll was kept.

"It's not much further now," said
Jasmine cheerfully. "We'll soon be at the
chalet. We'll get the scroll then head back
down to the village in time for the show."

They set off up the slope. The snow
was frozen hard and very slippery now,
and the girls' feet slid with every step.
They moved slowly, trying to keep their
balance.

Suddenly, Ellie slipped and fell over.
Summer and Jasmine made a grab for
her but they weren't quick enough and
she began to slide down the slope.

"Help!" Ellie cried. She scrabbled
frantically at the frozen snow, trying to
stop herself, but there was nothing to
hold on to.

"We're coming, Ellie!" called Summer.
Holding hands tightly, she and Jasmine

scrambled down the slope after their
friend.

But Ellie was sliding faster and faster
and heading straight for the ravine!

"Help!" she cried

again.

Then, to Summer and Jasmine's horror, Ellie reached the bottom of the slope – and plunged over the edge!

A New Friend

"Ellie!" Jasmine and Summer screamed.

To their relief, Ellie called back to them.
"I'm all right. I've landed on a ledge."
She sounded close to tears.

"We're coming," Summer shouted.
"Hang on."

"Please be quick," Ellie said, her voice
quavering with fear. "The ledge isn't very
wide and it's a really long way down."

Trixi and Dusty zoomed to the ravine

and hovered above it on their leaf and
snowflake. They tapped their rings and
chanted a spell:

"The snow is slippery. Our friend fell.
Return her to us safe and well."

A few sparkles trickled out of their
rings, but they faded almost at once.

"I'm so sorry, Ellie," Trixi said. "Our
magic still isn't working – Queen
Malice's curse is too strong."

Trembling, Ellie clung to a tree root
and shut her eyes. She didn't dare look
over the edge of the ledge. Just the
thought of the long drop below her made
her feel sick.

Summer and Jasmine finally reached
the edge of the slope. Holding on tightly

to the trunk of a fir tree so they wouldn't fall too, they looked down into the ravine. Ellie was kneeling on a narrow ledge about two metres down.

"Ellie, we're going to get you up," Jasmine called down to her.

"But how?" Summer whispered. "We

can't climb down – the side of the ravine's too steep."

"We need a rope," Jasmine said, "so we can pull her up."

Summer shook her head in despair. "We haven't got one." The wind sprang up. It lifted the end of Summer's scarf and flopped it over her face. "That's it!" Summer cried. "Scarves!" She pulled off her own. "If we tie our scarves together they'll be long enough to reach the ledge."

"That's a great idea!" exclaimed Jasmine. She hurriedly took off her scarf and gave it to Summer.

Summer quickly tied the ends of the two scarves tightly together. "There!" she said, when it was done. "This is just as good as a rope." She leaned over the edge of the ravine. "We're lowering a scarf rope down to you, Ellie. Tie it round your waist and we'll pull you up."

Jasmine secured one end of the scarf rope to the tree trunk and Summer dropped the other end down to Ellie.

Ellie took it with trembling hands and Trixi helped her tie the end around her body in a strong knot.

"Are you ready?" Summer called.

"I...I guess so," replied Ellie. She stood up shakily, her heart beating furiously.

Trixi hovered close beside her. "It's okay, Ellie. You'll be safe in no time," she said.

Jasmine and Summer took hold of the scarf rope. "One, two, three, pull!" said Summer. They hauled up the scarf rope, slowly lifting Ellie out of the ravine. It

was hard work,
but suddenly
her head and
shoulders
appeared over
the side. A
moment later she
was scrambling
up on to the
snowy slope. Jasmine
and Summer helped
her to her feet then
hugged her tightly.

"Thank goodness you're
okay," Jasmine said.

Ellie was pale and trembling, but the
colour soon came back to her cheeks.
"We can't stand around here all day," she
said, grinning at Summer and Jasmine.

"Let's go and find that scroll!"

They set off up the mountain again, holding on to the scarf rope so that if one of them slipped again the others would be able to stop them from sliding down the slope.

Suddenly, Jasmine heard a tinkling noise. "What's that?" she asked, looking round.

At first they couldn't see anything, then Summer spotted a bush shaking so hard that all the snow had fallen off its leaves. "Over there," she whispered, pointing.

"Is it the Hairy Snow Monster?" Dusty gulped.

"I don't think a monster would be wearing a bell," said Ellie. "Let's get a bit closer."

They crept towards the bush and

soon they could see that a little white
mountain goat had got her horns caught
in the branches. She was struggling to
detach them, and setting the bell around
her neck jingling.

The girls hurried forward to free her.

"Don't worry," Summer said, stroking
the goat's soft white
coat. "We'll soon
get you out."

Jasmine pulled
the branch
and it lifted a
little, letting
the goat

wriggle free. The goat skipped away in delight, then trotted back to nibble the end of the scarf rope.

The girls laughed.

"Goats will eat just about anything," said Summer with a giggle, shooing her away.

The goat trotted uphill, then stopped and glanced back at them. Bleating eagerly, she looked up at the chalet.

"I think she wants us to follow her," Summer said. "Maybe she knows an easier way to the top."

The goat cut across the slope to a path carved into the snow. It led all the way to the chalet's front door. The girls stepped on to it gratefully.

"This is great!" said Jasmine. "It's much less slippery."

They followed the goat uphill, walking
quickly to keep up with her.

"Keep an eye out for the monster,"
warned Dusty.

Suddenly, a snowball whizzed past
Ellie's ear.

Another whacked Jasmine on the chest
and smashed into a shower of powdery
snow. "Who threw that?" she gasped.

Looking up, the girls saw a large group
of Queen Malice's Storm Sprites further
up the mountainside. They were nasty,
ugly creatures with black bat-like wings
and sharp fingers.

"Ha, ha!" they jeered. "You'll never
make it to the top! The Hairy Snow
Monster will eat you first!" They threw
more snowballs, making the girls duck.

Suddenly, the goat gave a loud bleat.

She lowered her head and charged at
the nearest Storm Sprite as he bent down
to make another snowball. The goat
butted his bottom and sent him sprawling
in the snow.

Trixi laughed. "Serves you right!" she
cried.

The goat charged at a second sprite

and the rest of them took off in panic, their wings flapping frantically as they flew away.

The girls ran to hug the goat. "Thank you," they said.

The goat rubbed her silky head against their hands, then trotted on towards the chalet. The girls, Trixi and Dusty followed but as they reached the top of the peak they saw a sign that said BEWARE! in large red letters.

"It must be to warn people about the Hairy Snow Monster," Summer said anxiously.

"The goat doesn't seem scared," Jasmine said.

They went on and came to another sign saying STAY AWAY! The goat began to nibble the edge of it.

"You're right about goats eating anything, Summer." Ellie laughed. "This one even seems to like—" She broke off as a loud roar echoed through the cold air.

They all jumped, then clung together, looking round fearfully.

"Oh no!" squealed Dusty. "It's the Hairy Snow Monster!"

The Hairy Snow Monster

"What are we going to do?" gasped
Dusty. "The monster will eat us if he
catches us! They say he's got huge teeth
and claws and his fur is as white as the
snow, so you can't see him coming, even
though he's gigantic."

Summer shivered and looked round
nervously. Perhaps the monster was
hiding in the snow ahead, waiting for
them to come closer.

The roar sounded again, but it was impossible to tell where it was coming from because it echoed all around them.

The goat took another bite out of the sign.

"Why isn't the goat worried?" Jasmine said.

"Even if the monster is as big and scary as Dusty says, we can't give up now," Ellie said. "We've come all this way and if we don't find the Pixie Spell scroll, Queen Malice will win."

"You're right," said Summer determinedly. "We're almost at the chalet now. Let's keep going."

The goat trotted on towards the chalet and the girls, Trixi and Dusty followed her. They all kept a lookout for the monster, ready to flee if it appeared.

To their relief they reached the chalet
without being attacked by the monster.
The chalet was bigger than the houses
they'd seen in the village, but Jasmine still
had to bend down to knock on the door.

A fierce voice boomed, "I am the Hairy

Snow Monster. Go away!"

Dusty and Trixi shrieked and the girls grabbed each others' hands, their hearts thumping.

"Wait a minute," Ellie said, sounding puzzled. "A huge monster can't live in this chalet. It wouldn't fit through the door."

"That's right," agreed Summer. "*We'd* have to duck to get inside, so there's no way an enormous monster could fit."

"Let's find out who does live here," Jasmine said. She knocked again and called, "Please let us in!"

Nobody opened the door.

The goat disappeared round the corner of the chalet and bleated for them to follow.

As they crept round to the back of the chalet, the monster roared again, "Get away while you still can!"

A window at the back of the chalet was open. The girls tiptoed over to it and peered inside. An old elf with grey hair and glasses was shouting into a long wooden horn with a wide end. He was dressed in leather breeches, a patterned woolly waistcoat and a green hat with a feather in it. The horn was making his words come out in

a loud, echoing boom.

"Are *you* the Hairy Snow Monster?" Jasmine asked in astonishment.

The elf looked round, shocked, and dropped the horn. "Oh, dearie me," he said with a sigh. "You've found out my secret." His shoulders drooped and he looked very sad, but then he spotted the goat and his face lit up. "Snowbell!" he cried. He quickly opened the back door and ran outside to hug her. "Where have you been, you naughty girl? I've been so worried about you."

The goat bleated happily and nudged him gently with her nose.

"Her horns were caught in a bush," Ellie said. "But we managed to get them free."

"Thank you!" the elf exclaimed. "She's

been missing for two days and I thought
she was gone forever. She's my pet, you
see, and I love her dearly. Snowbell and I
look after the chalet together."

"Tell us about the Hairy Snow
Monster," said Dusty in a stern voice.

The elf sighed. "My name's Chilly,"
he said. "Come inside and I'll make
us all some hot drinks while I explain
everything."

The girls ducked through the low door,
then they and the pixies followed Chilly
and Snowbell into the chalet's cosy living
room, where a welcoming fire blazed in a
stone fireplace. The polished wooden floor
was dotted with white rugs and two large
sofas were piled high with cushions and
knitted blankets. Overflowing bookshelves
lined the walls, a spinning wheel stood

in front of the window and a large dog basket stood near the fire. Snowbell climbed into the basket and settled down on the cushions with a happy sigh.

Chilly heated some milk over the fire and made them all mugs of steaming hot chocolate. The girls took off their mittens and warmed their cold hands on their mugs as they sipped their drinks.

"You must love reading, with all these books," said Summer, gazing round as Chilly sat down in his armchair near the fire.

"I do. There's not much to do up here, with only Snowbell for company," the elf replied. "So I read, I spin wool and I knit." He patted a white cushion proudly. "I made all these cushions, blankets and rugs from Snowbell's wool."

"But why did you pretend to be the Hairy Snow Monster?" asked Dusty.

"The monster doesn't exist," Chilly replied. "It's an old story made up to

protect the kingdom's winter magic. A
very long time ago, one of King Merry's
ancestors thought Pixie Peak would be a
safe place to hide the Pixie Spell scroll."

"The final Enchanted Object!"
exclaimed Jasmine excitedly.

"Yes," Chilly agreed. "The spell scroll
is one of the four Enchanted Objects.
King Merry's ancestor had this chalet
built, brought the spell here and then
kept people away by spreading the story
of the Hairy Snow Monster. It's my job
to guard the spell, so I keep the monster
story going by putting up warning signs
and roaring into my horn." He smiled.
"I'm sorry if I scared you."

"We weren't scared one bit!" said Dusty,
winking and grinning at the girls and
Trixi.

"But what brings you girls all the way to the top of Pixie Peak?" asked Chilly.

"Queen Malice has put a curse on the kingdom to destroy all the good magic," said Summer.

"King Merry needs all of the Enchanted Objects to lift that curse," Ellie added.

"Can you give us the scroll?" asked Jasmine.

Chilly shook his head, frowning worriedly. "Oh dear. I unrolled the spell scroll and tucked it into a book to keep it extra safe…"

"Which book?" Summer asked quickly, jumping up and running to the nearest bookcase.

"That's the trouble. It was such a long time ago that I can't remember," said Chilly. His face turned red with embarrassment. "I know it was a silly thing to do, but it seemed like a good idea at the time."

"You were only trying to keep it safe," Ellie said, hoping to make him feel better.

"We'll help you search for it," said Summer. "What does it look like?"

It's very old and the paper's yellow with age," Chilly replied.

His clock whirred and a little wooden cuckoo popped out and chirped, "Cuckoo, cuckoo, cuckoo."

"It's three o'clock," said Dusty anxiously. "Almost time for the Winter Wonderland show to start."

"We have to find the spell quickly before the sand runs right through Queen Malice's timer," said Trixi.

They all jumped up and began flipping
through Chilly's books, searching for the
scroll.

"This is hopeless," Jasmine said with
a sigh. "There are so many books we'll

never find it in time."

"Hang on," said Summer suddenly. "Remember when we were looking for the Crystal Heart, Trixi? Your leaf was pulled towards its magic. Does it feel as though it's being pulled in any direction now?"

Trixi shook her head anxiously. "No," she replied. "The Pixie Spell's so powerful that its magic is filling the whole room. It's impossible to tell which book it's coming from and—" She broke off as a scratching sound came from the window.

"What was that?" asked Jasmine, running to the window. Frost covered the outside of the glass but she could just make out two shadows trying to scrape the frost away with their sharp fingers. "It's Storm Sprites!" she warned, jumping away from the window quickly. "They're trying to peer in!"

Pixie Spell

"The Storm Sprites mustn't find out about the Pixie Spell," whispered Ellie. "We'll have to get rid of them before we carry on searching for it."

"How, though?" asked Jasmine.

Ellie grinned. "The Hairy Snow Monster can help us."

"But it doesn't exist," Jasmine said, puzzled.

Ellie laughed. "The Storm Sprites don't know that." She quickly explained her plan and her friends started to grin.

Each grabbing an armful of blankets, the girls tiptoed out of the chalet's back door. Trixi and Dusty flew after them, and Chilly and Snowbell came, too. Chilly brought three pairs of snowshoes.

"Put these on," he said to the girls.

Summer picked up Snowbell, and Ellie and Jasmine stood on either side of her, squeezing up close and helping to hold the little goat.

Dusty and Trixi draped the fluffy white blankets over the girls and Snowbell. They tucked the blankets around Snowbell's horns so they poked out, then stood back to admire them.

"If I didn't know better, I'd say I was

definitely looking at the Hairy Snow Monster." Trixi giggled.

Jasmine peeped out from under the blankets. "We're ready now, Chilly."

The elf ran back indoors and boomed into his horn, "This is the Hairy Snow Monster! Go away!"

He went on shouting as Trixi and Dusty whizzed round to the front of the chalet.

"Help!" they screamed. "The Hairy Snow Monster's eaten our friends!"

The girls lumbered after them.

"I hope Snowbell doesn't give us away by bleating," Ellie said in a low voice.

"She's too busy eating my scarf," Summer whispered back.

As they reached the front of the chalet, the Storm Sprites spotted them.

"The Hairy Snow Monster!" they shrieked.

"I'm coming to get you!" Chilly boomed into his horn.

The girls tried not to laugh as they shuffled slowly towards the Storm Sprites.

The sprites flew into the air, their wings flapping madly. "Let's get out of here!" shouted one.

"The Hairy Snow Monster is scary," another sprite yelped.

The girls watched until the Storm Sprites were out of sight, then they collapsed into the snow.

"Did you see their faces?" hooted Jasmine.

Giggling, Summer pushed Snowbell away gently as the goat tried to nibble her hair.

Ellie suddenly remembered about the final Enchanted Object. "The Pixie Spell!" she cried. "We've got to find it quickly before the hourglass sand runs out!"

The girls pulled off their snow shoes and leapt up. Everyone raced back into the chalet.

"It's going to take ages to search every book," groaned Summer.

"I'll try using magic," said Trixi. "With the Enchanted Object so close, maybe if I do a spell, that will lead us to the scroll." She tapped her ring and chanted:

"The Pixie Spell's inside a book.
Show us where we need to look."

Glittering white light spilled out from the bookcase nearest the door.

"Look!" Ellie gasped. The spine of one of the books was glowing, and sparkles were fizzing around it.

Chilly beamed at Trixi. "Your spell worked," he said.

Summer lifted the book down carefully and a sheet of ancient paper floated out from its pages. It hovered in the air and a cloud of twinkling white dust puffed out

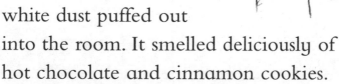

into the room. It smelled deliciously of hot chocolate and cinnamon cookies.

"The Pixie Spell!" said Dusty delightedly. "I never thought I'd see such a wonderful thing." She touched it gently with one finger and the white

dust turned sparkly pink. Then the paper
rolled itself back into a scroll.

Trixi glanced at Chilly's cuckoo
clock. "King Merry will be arriving in
the village for the start of the Winter
Wonderland Show very soon. We can
give him the Pixie Spell and end Queen
Malice's curse. Come on!"

They all ran outside where Trixi
quickly tapped her ring and chanted:

"The spell's been found, but time
is short.
Down the mountain we must go.
We need a large and speedy sledge
To whizz us all over the snow."

Sparkles came whooshing out of Trixi's
ring and spilled on to the snow. They

began to change into dancing snowflakes
and as they cleared the girls saw a tiny
red bobsled with gold runners in front of
the chalet.

"You'll be able to speed down the
mountain now," said Trixi. "Thank
goodness the Pixie Spell has restored my
ring's magic."

"Er, it's too small for us, Trixi," Ellie
said.

Trixi grinned. "Not for much longer."
She tapped her ring and silver sparkles
poured out and wreathed around the
girls, Chilly and Snowbell.

"We're shrinking!" cried Jasmine.

In a twinkling they were all pixie-sized
and fitted into the bobsled perfectly.

"You're small enough to enjoy the
Winter Wonderland Show properly now
too," Trixi said. "Hop in! There's no time
to lose!"

Jasmine sat in front and Ellie climbed in
behind her. Summer jumped in next and
Chilly sat at the back.

"Come on, Snowbell!" he cried, patting
a small space between him and Summer.

Bleating happily, the goat leapt into
the bobsled, snuggled up against Summer
and began to chew her scarf again.

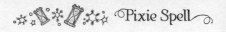

Trixi tapped her ring once more and
the bobsled whizzed away down the
mountain while she and Dusty
flew beside it.

"Whee!" cried Jasmine
as the sled gathered
speed.

"Going *down*
the mountain is
MUCH more fun
than going up
it!" shouted
Ellie as they
flew over
the snow.

The Winter Wonderland Show

"What an amazing ride!" gasped
Summer as the bobsled slid to a stop
in the middle of the village. But her
excitement didn't last long. Queen
Malice's magical hourglass loomed up
from the snow. The black sand had nearly
run through.

Winter Pixies crowded round to admire the bobsled, but there was no time for the girls to stop and chat. They had to get the Pixie Spell to King Merry as quickly as they could.

"Is the king here yet?" Jasmine asked the pixies as they jumped out of the bobsled.

Before anyone could reply, a giant rainbow appeared in the sky.

"King Merry's rainbow slide!" cried Ellie, pointing. The magical rainbow slide let the king travel around the Secret Kingdom quickly.

King Merry came sliding down the rainbow and landed in a patch of soft snow. He was wearing a purple ski suit with a gold, fur-trimmed cape and gold, fur-lined boots. Under his crown he wore a purple bobble hat.

"Greetings!" he cried, pushing his half-moon spectacles up his nose and beaming round at everyone. He struggled to his feet. To the girls, who were still pixie-sized, he looked like a giant.

Trixi tapped her ring and chanted:

"King Merry looks immensely tall.
Shrink him till he's pixie-small."

Rainbow-coloured sparkles poured out
of the ring and whizzed around King
Merry. When they vanished, he was just a
little bigger than the Winter Pixies.

"Good gracious!" he gasped, gazing at
the chalets all around in open-mouthed
astonishment. "Whatever's happened?" He
spun round, trying to look at everything
at once, and slipped over in the snow. His
crown flew one way and his glasses flew
the other.

The girls ran forward to help. Jasmine
and Summer quickly pulled him to his
feet while Ellie picked up the king's

crown and glasses. She hurriedly dusted
the snow off them
and handed
them back
to him.

"Thank
you,"
he said.
Putting
on his
glasses,
he looked at
the girls in surprise.
"Why, it's Ellie, Jasmine and Summer!
So wonderful to see you! Have you girls
found the fourth Enchanted Object?"

"Here it is, Your Majesty," said Jasmine.
"It's the Pixie Spell." She handed him the
scroll.

"There's no time to waste," Summer told him. "The sand in Queen Malice's hourglass has almost run through."

"Oh dear!" the king said anxiously. "Where's Trixi? She'll know what to do."

Trixi flew over to him, but before she could speak they heard the roar of an engine. Queen Malice came racing into the village on her snowmobile.

"Not so fast!" she screeched, taking off her crash helmet and flinging it down in the snow. She loomed over everyone, then snatched the hourglass from the snow and held it up. "Your time is almost up!" She made a grab for the scroll with her free hand, but King Merry held it behind his back. "Fine! Keep your silly Pixie Spell!" the queen shrieked. "The four Enchanted Objects are not back together

– so you've failed and I've won! In just a
moment, the sand in the hourglass will
run out, and the Secret Kingdom will
be mine!" She threw
back her head and
laughed nastily, her
black eyes flashing.

Hurriedly Trixi
tapped her ring
and chanted a
spell:

"The last Enchanted Object's here.
It must unite with the other three.
To end the mean queen's evil curse,
Have it join them, speedily!"

Golden sparkles poured out of the ring.
They whisked the Pixie Spell scroll out
of King Merry's hands and it suddenly
vanished.

The girls turned to look at the
hourglass. As the last grain of sand
dropped through, they held their breath.
Had the Pixie Spell reached the other
Enchanted Objects in time?

Suddenly the black sand inside the
hourglass began to change colour until
every last grain had become part of a
sparkling rainbow.

Then everyone looked up at Pixie

Peak as its summit began to glow with pink light. The light grew brighter and brighter, spreading down the mountain and changing colour until the snow, the rocks and the fir trees shone with every colour of the rainbow, too. Streams of colour spread out through the village, lighting every pathway and every snowy roof with sparkling brightness. The icicles that hung from eaves and balconies lit up as though a light had been switched on inside them. They threw out rays of emerald, gold, ruby and sapphire that set the whole village sparkling like a treasure chest of precious jewels.

The girls gazed round, spellbound.

"We did it!" breathed Jasmine. "Queen Malice's curse is broken!"

She, Summer and Ellie joined hands

and swung each other round in a circle.

"Our winter magic's back!" cheered a Winter Pixie, soaring high and looping the loop on her flying snowflake. Lots more pixies zoomed up into the sky, twirling round excitedly on their glittering snowflakes, their colourful

scarves streaming out behind them.

"You'll regret this!" screeched Queen
Malice, glowering at the girls. She leapt
on to her snow mobile and zoomed
away, leaving her crash helmet behind.
As she reached the edge of the village,
she looked back and shook her fist. The
snow mobile swerved, and crashed into
a snowbank. Queen Malice flew off
and landed head first in the mound of
snow. Her legs thrashed wildly, then she
pulled herself free and stood up. Her
black frizzy hair was completely covered
in white snow.

"Now that really *is* a scary Hairy Snow
Monster!" Jasmine chuckled.

The girls giggled as Queen Malice
tried to haul her snow mobile out of
the snowdrift, but it was stuck fast. She

thumped her
thunder staff
on the snow
angrily and
vanished.

"Thank
goodness
she's gone!"
Summer
cried.

Trixi flew
over. "It's time
for the Winter Wonderland Show," she
said, smiling. "King Merry would like you
to join him on the royal podium."

The girls hurried to a stage that had
been set up on one side of the village
square. King Merry was already sitting
on a golden throne with a purple blanket

over his lap. Chilly was sitting beside him under a green blanket and Snowbell was nibbling it happily.

"Welcome, my Very Important Friends!" King Merry called out as the girls settled into the comfortable chairs that had been set beside his throne. With a quick tap of her ring, Trixi conjured up a soft, warm blanket for each of them and a mug of steaming hot chocolate.

Snowbell suddenly spotted Summer and trotted over to eat what was left of her scarf.

"You've made a real friend there." Ellie giggled.

"Shh," whispered Trixi, as a group of young pixies lined up in front of the stage. "The show's about to start." She sat on the last chair, beside Jasmine.

The young Winter Pixies threw themselves backwards into the snow. They moved their arms and legs through the white powder and, as they stood up again, the girls saw that each of them had made a snow fairy. The pixies tapped their rings and the snow fairies came to life, fluttering up from the ground and soaring into the air. Their long white dresses twinkled dazzlingly and their wings shimmered as though they'd been sprinkled with glitter. As they flew higher and higher they began to sing in voices that sounded like the tinkling of tiny silver bells.

Next, snowmen began to march into the square, their scarves fluttering in the breeze. Some of them held flutes and drums and as the fairies' last notes died

away, they began to play. The other
snowmen formed circles, joining hands
and jigging round in time to the music.
The snowman that looked like King
Merry skipped around the edge of the
square, stopping to shake hands with
pixies in the crowd. The girls clapped

along to the beat of the drums, and Jasmine found herself itching to join in.

When the dance ended, everyone clapped and cheered as the snowmen bowed. Then the snow fairies swooped down again, bringing with them a garland of twinkling stars that they draped across the square.

"Now it's time for Dusty's flying display," said Trixi. She smiled nervously. "I hope she's okay. She's been so busy helping us that she hasn't had much chance to practise today."

Dusty whizzed into the square on her snowflake. She flew round, waving to the crowd, then soared high, her snowflake spinning and twisting skilfully. Finally she sprang into the air, turned three somersaults and landed neatly on her snowflake again.

The crowd applauded wildly.

Trixi leapt up. "Well done, Dusty!" she cried.

Dusty smiled and waved. King Merry stood up to clap. He was so excited he rushed forwards. "Oh, mittens and mufflers!" he cried as his foot caught in the blanket that had been on his lap. His arms flapped wildly as he struggled to keep his balance.

The girls darted forward and caught the little king before he fell. They set him

back on his feet again. Summer folded
the blanket and put it on his throne so he
wouldn't trip on it again.

"Thank you, my friends," murmured
the king. Then he moved to the front of
the stage and spoke to the crowd. "This
has been the most magical Wonder
Winterland, er...Winter Wonderland...
show ever! I would like to present a
special award to Dusty, for her bravery
and wonderful flying display. Come here,
my dear."

Blushing with pleasure, Dusty flew to
the stage and King Merry placed a gold
snowflake-shaped medal around her
neck. Snowbell gave an eager bleat and
darted forward to chew the ribbon.

"Oh no you don't!" Dusty laughed.
She zoomed up into the air where the

goat couldn't reach her.

A group of Winter Pixies stepped forward and tapped their rings, and the stars that the snow fairies had draped

across the square began to shine even more brightly. Suddenly they shot into the air and burst into thousands of tiny coloured stars, like fireworks. As the last star vanished, Trixi turned to the girls.

"That's the end of the show and it's time for you to go home. Thank you so much for saving the Secret Kingdom's magic."

The girls quickly said goodbye to King Merry, Dusty, Chilly and Snowbell, then they held hands and Trixi tapped her ring. Instead of sparkles,

glittering snowflakes came whooshing
out. They spun around the girls, lifting
them off their feet. "Goodbye," they
called. "See you again soon."

A moment later they landed in
Summer's bedroom, back to their normal
size once more.

"Isn't it nice to know that the Secret
Kingdom's magic will be working

properly next time we go there?" Summer said happily as she hid the Magic Box under her bed.

"Definitely," agreed Jasmine and Ellie together.

As usual, time had stood still while they were having their adventure.

"We need to get back to our homework," Ellie said. "Have you chosen an animal habitat for your project yet, Summer?"

Summer grinned. "High snowy lands," she said, "and mountain goats!"

In the next Secret Kingdom adventure, Ellie, Summer and Jasmine become

Royal Bridesmaids

Read on for a sneak peek...

A Special Invitation

"Would anyone like a chocolate chip cookie?" Mrs Macdonald called up the stairs.

Ellie and her best friends, Summer and Jasmine, jumped to their feet. They were playing snap in Ellie's bedroom but they weren't going to turn down one of Ellie's mum's freshly-baked biscuits.

"Race you downstairs!" Ellie said.

They all charged downstairs and burst into the kitchen. Molly, Ellie's little sister, was sitting at the kitchen table with a cookie in her hand, looking through some old photo albums. With her curly red hair, freckles and green eyes, she looked just like a mini version of Ellie.

"Help yourselves, girls," said Mrs Macdonald, offering a plate of cookies.

"Yum! Thank you!" said Summer, as she bit into a still-warm cookie.

"You make the best cookies, Mrs Macdonald," Jasmine said.

Mrs Macdonald smiled. "Thanks, Jasmine."

"What are you doing, Molly?" Ellie asked, going over to her sister.

"I've got to take some photos into

school," said Molly. "We're doing a project about our families. I've got to take some pictures in of you and Mum and Dad and some of me when I was a baby."

Ellie giggled at the picture of her parents' wedding. "Look at Dad's hair!" It was spiky on top and long at the back. "I'm glad he doesn't look like that any more."

Her mum grinned back. "Me too! But it was stylish at the time."

"I love weddings," said Summer with a sigh, looking at the photos over Ellie's shoulder. Ellie's mum was wearing a white lace wedding dress in the photos and a headdress made of flowers. "Your dress was really beautiful."

"I made it myself," Ellie's mum said.

"We didn't have much money so I made my dress and the bridesmaids' dresses and the cake. We had a wonderful day."

"Did you have dancing after the wedding?" Jasmine asked. She loved dancing.

"We did," said Mrs Macdonald. "We danced all night." Her eyes glowed as she remembered it. "It was so much fun."

"I wish I could go to a wedding," said Ellie. "I've never been to one."

"I was a bridesmaid once but I was too little to remember it," said Jasmine.

"Imagine if we could all go to a wedding and be bridesmaids together," said Summer.

Molly turned the pages of the photo album. "Look at Ellie!"

The girls all giggled. It was a picture

of Ellie as a baby. She was lying on a changing mat with just a nappy on. She had no hair, huge green eyes and chubby legs and arms. "I was a really roly-poly baby!" Ellie said.

"You were the cutest baby in the world," her mum said fondly.

"What about me?" Molly said indignantly.

"OK, you were *both* the cutest babies in the world," said Mrs Macdonald. "Let's find some pictures of you now, Molly."

"I can't believe I looked like that when I was a baby," said Ellie as they went back upstairs to her room. "My tummy was almost as tubby as King Merry's!"

"No one's tummy could be as round as King Merry's," said Summer.

King Merry was the ruler of the Secret

Kingdom, a magical land that only Ellie, Summer and Jasmine knew about. They had been there lots of times and met all sorts of amazing people and creatures – tiny pixies and giant dream dragons, beautiful unicorns and cuddly snow bears.

"It's been ages since we last went to the Secret Kingdom," said Jasmine. "Let's check the Magic Box. There might be a message for us."

Whenever King Merry wanted the girls to come to the Secret Kingdom, a riddle appeared in the Magic Box's mirrored lid. Ellie knelt down on the floor. There were two big wicker baskets under her bed and she started to pull one out. "I put the Magic Box in here to keep it—" She broke off with a gasp as sparkling light flooded out.

"The Magic Box is glowing!" said Summer.

"There must be a message! Quick, Ellie!" said Jasmine.

Ellie took the Magic Box out of the basket. A riddle was scrolling across its lid. Her heart raced as she read out the words.

"Where parties are held and sweet bubbles fly, King Merry awaits where pink turrets reach high!"

Read

Royal Bridesmaids

to find out what
happens next!

Have you read all the books in Series Seven?

When the last grain of sand falls in Queen
Malice's cursed hourglass, magic will be lost
from the Secret Kingdom forever!
Can Ellie, Summer and Jasmine find all the
Enchanted Objects and break the spell?

Keep all your dreams and
wishes safe in this gorgeous
Secret Kingdom Notebook!

Includes a party planner, diary, dream
journal and lots more!

Out now!

Secret Kingdom

Look out for the latest special!

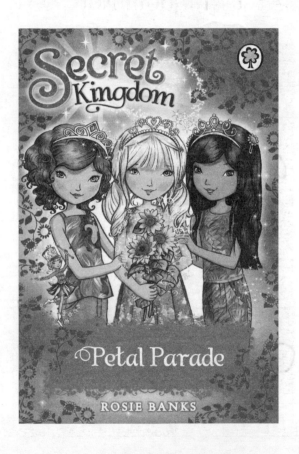

Out now!

Secret Kingdom

Queen Malice's spell on the Magic Hourglass is making everything in the Secret Kingdom go wonky!

Can you help the girls put things right by finding the six missing words in the word search below?

Shell   Trixi

Pearl   Mermaid

Manatee   Magic

G	L	K	F	P	O	Y	X	H	P
J	W	I	E	E	S	I	Q	K	O
I	M	A	N	A	T	E	E	S	L
T	R	H	X	R	F	U	N	H	F
E	N	A	R	L	Y	B	S	E	B
L	R	J	Y	I	I	M	I	L	N
D	U	L	O	E	E	A	L	L	M
A	H	A	N	S	D	G	D	E	R
F	M	E	R	M	A	I	D	I	P
L	I	M	T	C	S	C	E	R	H
I	M	E	S	T	R	I	X	I	O

Competition!

Those naughty Storm Sprites are up to no good again. They have trampled through this book and left muddy footprints on one of the pages!

Did you spot them while you were reading this book?

Can you find the pages where the cheeky sprites have left their footprints in each of the four books in series 7?
When you have found all four sets of footprints, go online and tell us which pages they are on to enter the competition at

www.secretkingdombooks.com

We will put all of the correct entries into a draw and select a winner to receive a special Secret Kingdom goody bag!

Alternatively send entries to:
Secret Kingdom, Series 7 Competition
Orchard Books, Carmelite House, 50 Victoria Embankment, London, EC4Y 0DZ

Don't forget to add your name and address.

Good luck!

Closing date: 29th February 2016

Secret Kingdom

A magical world of friendship and fun!

Join the Secret Kingdom Club at

www.secretkingdombooks.com

and enjoy games, sneak peeks and lots more!

You'll find great activities, competitions, stories
and games, plus a special newsletter for
Secret Kingdom friends!